Mickey the Monkey

Mickey the Monkey

By
Adèle and Cateau De Leeuw

Illustrated by
Robert Henneberger

Little, Brown and Company
Boston ... 1952

Published simultaneously
in Canada by McClelland and Stewart Limited

PRINTED IN THE UNITED STATES OF AMERICA

Mickey the Monkey

Chapter One

Tom looked up from the book he was reading, and there on the window sill sat a monkey!

He could hardly believe his eyes. This was the day his class was going to the Zoo on an outing — a chartered bus, a picnic lunch, rides on the elephants and camels and a tour to see all the animals. And *he* had a cold.

He had been thinking about it so hard all morning that maybe he was dreaming. He stared at the monkey, and the monkey stared back. Then a tiny gray paw knocked on the pane.

"Let me in!" the monkey called.

There was no doubt about it. That was what he said in a small clear voice. It came again, this time louder and more impatient. "Let me in!"

Tom opened the window and the monkey leaped lightly onto the floor. "Well," he said, shaking himself, "I thought you'd never open it."

"Where did you come from?" Tom asked, thinking of all the stories he had read about monkeys in Africa and South America and India. This monkey had tiny hands and feet and little ears and gray fur and his eyes snapped in his lined, old-man's face.

"Where did I come from? From Dr. Dinkelhofer's, down the street," he said. "What's your name?"

"Tom," said Tom. "What's yours?"

"Mine's Mickey. . . . Why are you sitting here all cooped up on a day like this?"

"I'm supposed to have a cold," Tom told him.

Mickey said quickly, "Supposed to? *Do* you have one or don't you?"

"Mother says I still have and the others might catch it, but *I* think it's over," Tom said. He told Mickey

[4]

about his big disappointment. "It would have been such fun to go to the Zoo — "

"I've always wanted to see all those animals myself," Mickey said. "Particularly if the big ones are safe in cages." He curled his tail around his body and sat straight. His eyes glittered. "Listen. Why don't we go together?"

Tom leaped up, grinning, his cold forgotten. "Let's! I've got some money — " He ran over to his desk and took down his airplane bank. It was so full he had a hard time getting the money out, but he shook and shook and shook, and the coins dropped out one by one. When he gathered them all up and counted them they came to eighty-seven cents. You could do a lot with eighty-seven cents.

Then Tom emptied the things out of his pocket, just to be sure they were all there. Mickey jumped up on the chair and watched him stuffing them back. There was a slingshot, and a couple of marbles, and some nails, and a long piece of rolled-up string, and a knife, and a handkerchief, and a package of peppermints.

"I'd get tired carrying all that around," Mickey said. "Why don't you leave it here?"

"Oh no," Tom said hurriedly. "Some of it might come in handy; you never can tell."

"Well, I'm glad *I* don't have to carry it. . . . What are we waiting for?"

"You go out of the window again," Tom said, "so I can close it the way it was. I'll meet you out back."

He wanted to tell his mother where he was going, but she was nowhere in sight, and he hadn't time to look for her. Anyhow, he knew his way, and he had money and supplies. He closed the back door very softly, and ran down the steps.

Mickey was jumping up and down, his wizened little face screwed up anxiously. "I thought you were never coming," he said. He reached for Tom's hand. "Do you know your way?"

"Oh, sure."

"It's more than I do."

"You can always ask," Tom told him.

"No, I can't," Mickey said. "That is, I can ask, but if nobody understands me, what's the use?"

Tom was struck by a sudden thought. "*I* understand you. I did right away. And you understood me!"

"That's because we like each other," Mickey answered quickly.

Yes, Tom decided, that must be it. He had liked Mickey the moment he had seen him huddled on the sill, and Mickey must have felt the same way about him.

He clutched Mickey's tiny hand tighter and said, "We'll take a bus. It's too far for you to walk."

"I can walk as far as you can," Micky protested.

But the big green bus was coming around the corner just then, and Tom waved for it to halt.

He started up the steps with Mickey behind him, and handed the driver two nickels.

"This nickel's for me, and this is for Mickey."

"Mickey?" the driver asked, laughing. "And where is he now? Invisible-like, or hidin' under your shirt?"

Tom stepped aside, and the driver saw the monkey. He scowled and his voice changed. "Tryin' to be funny, are ye? No ANIMALS ALLOWED, says the company, and NO ANIMALS it is."

[7]

"That's silly," Mickey said. "*People* are animals, and the bus is full of them."

Tom thought that was very sensible, and he looked admiringly at Mickey. But the bus driver hadn't seemed to hear him.

Tom explained, "Mickey says, 'People are animals, and the bus is full of them.' And I say so, too. So why can't Mickey ride if I pay for him?"

Mickey jumped up on Tom's shoulder where he could lean down and shake his little paw in the conductor's face.

"And it's lip you're both givin' me, is it?" the driver said loudly. "Now that's enough, and no more palaverin'. Off with ye — I don't want any more nonsense, and what I say goes."

Now that Mickey was up on Tom's shoulder, the bus passengers could see him for the first time. There was a sudden commotion. "Take it out! Take it away!" two women shrieked, right up front. The others craned their necks; one old lady cowered behind her hands, another one made shooing motions, and a man started forward with a folded-up newspaper.

"Let's get out of here," Tom said. "They don't seem to like us."

"That goes double," said Mickey, and snatched the bus driver's cap from his head. They swung off the bus and began to run.

[9]

The driver let out a yell that could be heard down the block and started after them. But at that the passengers began to shout, too. "Come back! Come back! Don't you dare leave your bus!"

The driver muttered and hesitated. In that moment Tom and Mickey put on an extra burst of speed and got away safely. "I won't be forgettin' this," the driver shouted after them. "You young rapscallions, you, wait till I get my hands on the both of ye!"

Tom was troubled. "Oh gleeps, you shouldn't have done that! Maybe the police will be after us now."

"Don't worry," Mickey retorted. "I never saw the police, but I can handle them. No ANIMALS ALLOWED, indeed! That fellow needed a lesson."

He put the dark blue cap with its gold cord and brass shield on his head and it nearly covered it. Tom laughed out loud, and Mickey pushed the cap back and grinned at him. His little old-man's face was all puckered up with amusement, and his tiny hands held the cap on firmly.

"Let me carry it," Tom said. "It's too big for you."

"I'll get used to it," Mickey assured him. He placed

it carefully on the back of his neck and peered out from the overhanging visor.

"Have you got your two nickels?" he asked.

"Yes. He never did take them."

"Well, that's all right then." The bus had driven off in a spurt of smoke and gasoline fumes, and Mickey cavorted beside him. "That was fun. . . . Nothing like this ever happens at Dr. Dinkelhofer's. I get *so bored*."

"Doesn't he ever play with you?"

"*Play* with me?" Mickey gave a queer little snort. "I don't think the man knows how to play . . . not with me, anyhow. No, he's studying me."

"What for?"

"He's writing a book on monkey behavior, he says," Mickey sighed. "Oh dear, if he'd only get done with it, so I could act natural!"

"But why can't you act natural, even if he's writing a book?"

"He has ideas," Mickey said patiently. "You know — about what monkey behavior should be. So he keeps peering at me, and noting everything down in a little book, and I have to think twice before I do anything so it'll look like what the professor thinks is monkey behavior!"

Mickey looked so dejected that Tom burst out laughing.

"It's no laughing matter," Mickey said with annoyance, scurrying along beside Tom. "How would *you* like to have somebody looking at you when you ate and played and slept and just *sat* — somebody who was trying to figure out if you were being a normal monkey — I mean, boy — and looking worried if you did something that he thought you shouldn't do?"

"I know what you mean," Tom said with sympathy.

Mickey stopped short. "You *do?*" he asked, his eyes bright.

"Yes, parents are like that sometimes," Tom said.

"Well, well." Mickey sounded very surprised. "I never thought of that. I suppose we all have our troubles."

Chapter Two

It was a long way to the Zoo, but they finally got there. Not many people were on the streets, and those they passed didn't seem to notice anything peculiar about a boy out walking with a monkey. When Tom mentioned it Mickey grinned. "Maybe they think I'm taking *you* for a walk."

The Zoo had a high fence all around it so you couldn't see inside. Cars were parked along the fence, and there too was the yellow school bus, empty.

"I'll buy the tickets," Tom began, but Mickey said:

"Buy your own. I won't need any. I'll just skitter over the fence."

And before Tom could say another word, he had leaped up the board fence, as quick as a wink. "See you inside!" he called from the top, and disappeared from view.

Tom hurried through the wicket and there sat Mickey, huddled in the shadow of the gatekeeper's little house. It looked as if they had the Zoo almost to themselves. It was a gloomy fall day and rather chilly, and not many people were out. There wasn't even a sign of his classmates, and Tom thought they must be nearly through with their tour and ready for the picnic lunch. It was hard to know where to go first, because there were so many things he wanted to see.

Mickey decided it for him. "The elephants are over there," he said, pointing. "I can smell them."

"I can't," Tom said, sniffing.

"That's because you're not a monkey."

"Does everything have a smell? Do people?" Tom wanted to know.

"Of course. You, too. That's why I picked you. You smelled all right."

Tom said, after a moment, "Come to think of it, how did you ever get out of Dr. Dinkelhofer's in the first place? And how did you find me?"

"Oh, that was easy," Mickey said airily. He pushed up the cap which kept sliding down over his head. He had to keep his neck back so that it would stay on at all, but he didn't seem to mind. "I have a big cage in a room in his house, and an old man takes care of me. That is, he *thinks* he takes care of me, but I could do better by myself. He's as slow as a sloth when he moves. So today, when I got so bored I couldn't stay there another minute, I just rapped on the wall, and he thought it was somebody knocking. When he went to see, I reached through the bars and undid the catch — "

"That was clever," Tom interrupted.

"Well, I'd been watching him use it every day for months," Mickey said. "Why wouldn't it be easy? And I ran to the window which was open and slid down the drainpipe. . . . Silly things, drainpipes."

"Why?"

"Why? What are they for?"

"For monkeys to slide down, I guess," Tom said, laughing. "Then what did you do?"

"Oh, I climbed a big tree and swung along from one tree to the next and looked in the windows as I went along. In one a man was sitting dozing in a chair, so I knew he wouldn't be any fun, and in another a lady was shaking out a broom, and I didn't like *that,* and in another a baby was crawling around, and finally I came to your house. You looked all right and you smelled all right, so I sat on your ledge till you saw me. My, it took you a long time! Was it a good book?"

"Not very," Tom said. "I guess I was just thinking — and wishing . . ."

They had come to the elephant house and Mickey quivered with excitement.

"Wait," said Tom, darting off to a stand down the path. "I must get some peanuts."

When he came back Mickey was sitting on the elephant's forehead and waving his arms. "Look at me!"

he cried, and with that he slid down the elephant's trunk, just as if he were sliding down a banister, and landed with a little plop in the bus driver's cap which he had set, bottom side up, on the ground. "Whee!" he said, hopping out. "That was a wonderful free ride! It took my breath away!"

The elephant's little piggy eyes were all screwed up as if he were laughing. Tom and Mickey fed peanuts to him; Tom liked the way the elephant took them, ever so gently, out of his palm, and curved his trunk upward and inward. One after another they disappeared till Mickey said suddenly, "Hey! I could use some of these myself!"

After they left the elephant Mickey darted dizzily over the ground, zigzagging about so quickly that Tom could barely keep up with him. "Now *there's* a ride I'd like!" he cried, pointing to a giraffe, its head lost in a clump of leaves high above his cage. "Wait till I climb up this tree —"

"No!" Tom said firmly and grabbed him by the hand.

"Why not?" Mickey argued. "He can't make a

sound; it would be quite safe. I could be up there in a minute."

"No," said Tom, still more firmly. "Come on, I want to see the hippopotamus. . . . I just learned how to spell it."

"Well, if you can see it why do you have to learn to spell it?"

"Here," said Tom, "have another peanut. You can ask the queerest questions!"

Just then the hippopotamus waddled out of his trough and came toward them. Its reddened eyes blinked crossly and it opened its mouth — wide, WIDE, wider, WIDER . . .

Mickey leaped up on Tom's shoulder and cowered behind his head. "I don't like it, I don't like it, I don't like it," he chattered. "Let's go away from here."

"He can't get out," Tom said, feeling very old and wise. "And anyhow, he's only yawning."

"That's what *you* say." Mickey was still chattering with fear.

"All right," Tom said, "we'll move on. I don't care much for his looks, either. But I'm not afraid of him."

"Oh, I'm not *afraid*," Mickey said. Now that they were some distance from the hippopotamus he acted much braver. "It's just that I think he would look better if he kept his mouth closed." He ran around Tom's back to his other shoulder and down his arm to the ground. "Did you eat all the peanuts?"

"Here," said Tom, fishing in his pocket, "finish this bag. I finished the other one."

Mickey began shelling the nuts, strewing the path with the shells. Tom looked around fearfully. "Listen," he said, "why don't you put the shells in the cap and then when we come to a can marked RUBBISH we'll throw them in?"

"Are peanut shells rubbish?"

"Yes."

"Then why don't they mark the can PEANUT SHELLS?"

"Because," said Tom patiently, "there's other rubbish. Peanut shells aren't the only kind."

"I could put them in my cheek."

"No," said Tom, "put them in the cap."

"But I can't hold the cap and get the shells off, too."

"I'll hold the cap, then," Tom offered.

"I'd rather keep the cap," Mickey said distrustfully, "and you shell the nuts."

"Oh," Tom cried, "there's a zebra! Doesn't he look as if he had leaned against a picket fence that had just been painted?"

"A picket fence?" Mickey was puzzled. "What's that?"

"A thing that looks like the side of a zebra," Tom said easily. "D'you know why he's marked like that?"

"Because he leaned up against a picket fence that had just been painted," Mickey said brightly.

Tom laughed. "You say the funniest things! They're marked that way so they can go through the forest without being seen."

"Does a picket fence have to go through a forest, too, without being seen?" Mickey inquired.

"Never mind," Tom sighed. "Do you know what that is over there?"

Mickey looked where Tom was pointing. "It's Dr. Dinkelhofer's hatrack," he announced.

"It's a *moose*," Tom corrected.

"Maybe so," Mickey said, "but Dr. Dinkelhofer has one just like that in his hall." He had a sudden idea. "I know — I'll hang my cap on his horns and show you."

Tom pulled him along. "Not now — when we come back maybe. I want to see the monkey house."

"No," said Mickey, "not there."

"Why not?"

"Are they in cages?"

"Yes. . . . Oh," Tom said quickly, "I see. Well, we won't go there, then. After all, I have *you,* and you're better than a whole houseful of monkeys. More fun, too."

"That's because I'm not in a cage," Mickey said. "Why, for goodness' sake, there's an animal with a pocket in its front!"

"That's a kangaroo," Tom told him. It was very pleasant being able to tell things to Mickey; it made him feel as if he knew a great deal. "She carries the little kangaroos in there."

"What's the matter, can't they walk by themselves?"

"Well, when she carries them they can get places faster."

"There aren't any little kangaroos in it now,"
Mickey observed. "What does she put in it then?"
He looked hopefully at Tom. "We could put the
peanut shells —"

"No, no," Tom said hurriedly, "she wouldn't like
that. We'll find a rubbish can soon."

"There ought to be something in that pocket of
hers," Mickey said thoughtfully. Then his face bright-

ened. "What's the matter with *me?*" And with the words he dropped the cap and was over the fence and running toward the kangaroo.

Tom called to him to come back, but Mickey did not seem to hear. He hopped into the pocket so quickly that the kangaroo was startled and bounded off to the other end of her enclosure. Tom could see Mickey's head bouncing up and down over the edge of the pocket, and he even thought he heard a faint voice crying, "Oh — oh — make her stop!"

The kangaroo circled along the fence in great leaps. Suddenly she paused, as if she were thinking of jumping the fence itself, and instantly a ball of gray fur tumbled to the ground. Mickey staggered toward Tom and climbed the fence in a groggy fashion. At the top he huddled a moment, clutching his stomach with both hands.

"Why, oh why, did I ever do that? I feel terrible!"

Tom said, "I told you not to, but you wouldn't listen. Here, have a peanut."

"Don't mention food to me," Mickey groaned. "Not till my insides get straightened out."

[24]

He climbed down slowly and picked up the cap with its peanut shells. "Where do we go now?" Already he seemed better. And Tom, casting a backward glance, thought the kangaroo looked relieved, too.

"Let's go to see the sea lions," he suggested. "It must be about time for them to be fed. I can hear them barking."

On the way they passed the bats and the hyenas, the lion house — from which came a terrifying roar — and the camels. "When one of those gets hungry and thirsty on the desert and there's no food, he uses up what is in his hump," Tom told Mickey, but Mickey looked thoughtful.

"How does he use it up? He can't eat it. His neck isn't long enough to get his mouth back there. He ought to have his hump in front."

"That isn't the way camels are made," Tom said. "Some kinds have *two* humps."

"Then they can get twice as hungry," Mickey reasoned.

They had come to the big tank where the sea lions lived. Tom and Mickey stood, fascinated, while the

sleek, shining wet creatures curved in the air, cleverly catching the fish thrown to them by the keeper and slipping off into the water with them and then, almost at once, coming back for more. It was chilly by the tank and people drew their coats closer about them.

Mickey shivered. "Oooh, look at that poor man," he cried, "with no fur on his head, and a day like this!" Tom started to giggle but thought better of it. The bald man was standing right beside them. At first he was afraid the man might have overheard Mickey and would not like to be talked about that way, but then he remembered that nobody could understand what Mickey said — only he himself.

The man looked rather cross. He had a short, squatty figure and a scowl on his red face; but his head wasn't red at all — it was white and shiny and it did look very uncomfortable.

"He's bald," Tom said, very low, so the man couldn't hear. "He did have hair on his head one time, but he lost it."

"Where?"

"I don't know. Lots of men lose their hair . . . it just falls out, I guess."

"It must be awful not to have fur — I mean, hair — on your head," Mickey said sadly. "Why doesn't he put something on it? Poor man! Animals never lose their head fur. . . ." He looked down at the cap he still held. As quick as a wink he leaped to the guard rail, clambered over the man's arm, and plunked the bus driver's cap on the bald man's head.

[27]

It landed half over one eye. Peanut shells fell over his face, and one piece caught on his bushy eyebrows. They rolled down his nose and down his neck and into his collar. He snatched off the cap and let out a roar that sounded as loud as a lion's.

"You little devil!" he bellowed. "I'll get you for this!"

"Oh, now you've done it!" Tom groaned. "Run, Mickey, run!"

The two of them turned and fled as fast as their legs could carry them, the man in hot pursuit. They raced over the path, around the lion house, past the birds and the tapirs and the wolves and the brown bears. They skirted the peanut stand, nearly knocking it over.

"Quick, Mickey, he's gaining on us!"

"Over the fence!" Mickey gasped.

"It's too high for me. Through the gate!"

They skittered past the band-stand and the snakes and the ducks and the deer. The gate — at last! Tom was winded, his heart beat like a hammer. They tore through the revolving wickets, while the ticket taker woke from a doze and yelled after them. "Run for that car," Tom panted. "Around the corner . . . behind the tree. See it?"

They made it together. Tom wrenched open the back door. They fell onto the floor, breathing hard,

and pulled an old tarpaulin over them. Neither one spoke for a few seconds. They just listened. There were no following footsteps.

"We've lost him," Tom said happily.

"Pooh, he couldn't run — he was too fat," Mickey said. "Let's get out of here, it's so hot I can hardly breathe."

"No, no. . . . Lie still. We'll stay here a bit; he might be hunting for us. Then we can get out."

Mickey crouched companionably close to Tom. "It was fun, wasn't it?" He sounded as if he were chuckling. "I'll never forget the way he looked with those peanut shells all over him! It was much better than putting them in the rubbish can!"

"*Sssh!*" Tom hissed. "Be quiet. Someone's coming."

Chapter Three

THE FOOTSTEPS were slow and heavy. Tom and Mickey crouched under the tarpaulin, waiting for them to pass. But they did not pass. They stopped at the car, the front door was yanked open, and the person got in. Tom was sure it was a man; he sounded old and stout, somehow, and as if he were tired.

There was a series of sputters, then the engine caught with a roar, and the whole car shook and rattled. Suddenly it gave a shudder that flung Tom and Mickey against the back of the front seat, and the car moved off, coughing and stuttering and humping itself like a camel.

"Whew! I don't like the smell of this thing," Mickey said, hitting at the tarpaulin with his little hands. "Let's get out."

"We can't."

"Well, where are we going?"

"I wish I knew," Tom said mournfully.

He didn't like the smell of the tarpaulin, either, and he was as hot as Mickey. But he didn't dare stick his head out yet — at any moment the man might turn around and see them. And if he saw who they were, he might return them to the Zoo. My, that had been a narrow escape! His heart still raced with all his running, and the excitement of being chased.

The car stopped . . . for only a moment; and then started up again, wheezing and puffing.

"That was a red light," Tom said, in the darkness.

Mickey wanted to know how he knew and he said, "Because we stopped and started again. . . . Here's another. So we must still be in town."

After a little while the car seemed to settle down to a steady pace. It made so much noise he could hardly think, but still it kept going and the riding was fairly smooth. "We must be out of town on the highway," Tom decided.

"Can we get out now?" Mickey asked hopefully, lifting an edge of the tarpaulin and starting to crawl forth.

Tom pulled him back. "Not yet!" he ordered firmly. "How do we know where we are?"

"How are we going to find out if we don't look?" Mickey asked. It sounded reasonable, but Tom ruled against it. They must still wait a while. "When the car stops we'll get out," he said.

They didn't stay on the highway long. The car swerved to the right and immediately began to joggle and bounce, throwing them about on the floor in a higgledy-piggledy fashion. Tom could feel Mickey bouncing onto his chest, and then *he* rolled over onto Mickey and Mickey said "Eeeek!" so loudly that Tom instantly rolled back again and put his hand over Mickey's mouth. Mickey nibbled at his fingers.

"We're in the country now," Tom said importantly. "It must be a dirt road."

"And not a good one, either," Mickey said crossly. "I'll be black and blue if we don't soon stop."

"Under your fur?" Tom asked, trying to picture it.

"Well, not on top!" Mickey said, still crossly, and Tom began to giggle. Instantly Mickey's small hand was over *his* mouth. "Who's making a noise now?" he asked.

And with that the car stopped.

It was such a relief that neither one could believe it. They waited for the joggling and jouncing to start up again, but it didn't. A car door slammed, and they realized that the driver had gotten out and was walking away. It seemed very quiet after all the noise.

With one accord, Tom and Mickey threw off the heavy tarpaulin and raised themselves up so they could look through the window.

The man was walking toward the house. He was short and stout. And he was bald!

They had ridden all that way behind the very man who had chased them at the Zoo! What would he have done if he had known that the boy and the monkey he had chased were in the back of his car all the time?

The bald-headed man crossed the yard with his short, waddly steps. Halfway across he stopped and reached up and scratched his neck and shook himself. A peanut shell rolled out of his collar.

"What are we going to do now?" Tom asked.

"Let's get out and look around," Mickey said. "Since we're here, we might as well." He climbed up on top of the front seat and peered over. "The cap!" he cried joyfully, and snatched it to him.

Tom opened the car door very cautiously. "We'd better not make any noise."

"They're making so much themselves they couldn't hear *us*," Mickey observed. Tom listened. It was true. From the house came voices — the man's, and then a woman's, and then both together. As they stood still they could hear the words.

"And I tell you, I was standing there as quiet as you please when all of a sudden a monkey clapped a cap full of peanut shells on my head!" the man was saying.

The woman snorted. "I thought you said you were looking at the sea lions."

"I was!"

"I suppose the monkey was just running around loose!"

"Well, no, he was with a boy. . . . I chased the two of them all over the grounds —"

"And what did you do with them when you caught them?" his wife interrupted.

"I didn't catch them — they ran too fast for me. I'd have got them in another minute if they hadn't disappeared, just like that! Nobody could find hide nor hair of them!"

"John Henry Coates, you're making it all up out of whole cloth — "

"I'll prove it to you if you won't believe it!" he shouted. "I have that cap right out there on the car seat. . . . Wait till I get it."

"I'll go with you," she said grimly. "How do I know you won't disappear again?"

Tom and Mickey scurried around the corner of the house as the man and woman came out of the back door. Their angry voices floated back. The man opened the car door and reached in. Then a strange, baffled expression spread over his face. Mickey put his little hand over his mouth and snickered.

"It — it isn't there!" the man cried, turning, bewildered, to his wife. "It isn't there!"

Chapter Four

Tʜᴇ ᴡᴏᴍᴀɴ sᴛᴏᴏᴅ with her hands on her hips. "Just as I thought!" she said, thinning her lips. "I don't believe you went to the Zoo in the first place! A boy with a monkey running around loose indeed! Planting a cap full of peanut shells on your head indeed! You come back to the house with me and change into your work-clothes this minute. There's a raft of things to be done about this place."

She took him firmly by the shoulder and propelled him back to the house. Mickey covered his ears. "Rackety-rackety-rackety-rack," he said. "How people can talk! If that's what he has to live with, I'm sorry for him. Maybe *she* made him bald!"

"If you'd left the cap on the seat beside him, she would have believed him," Tom said reproachfully to Mickey.

"I don't think so. She doesn't believe anybody. . . ." He placed the cap carefully on the back of his neck and began walking about with his old proud air. "Let's look around while we're here. . . . But I don't think we'd better stay."

"We're safe for a while, I guess," Tom decided. "She said she had a lot for him to do."

"It doesn't look as if he ever did much about the house," Mickey said with a critical air, cocking his head. "Nor about the grounds or barn, either."

No, thought Tom, it didn't. The house needed paint badly and the back porch steps sagged. There were pieces of rusty metal lying around the yard, and he re-membered how the car had rattled and wheezed. The barn had shingles missing from the roof, and there was a pile of junk beside the chicken house. But there were red and gold leaves on the trees, and windfall apples and green-husked nuts on the ground, and an autumn blue sky overhead. It had cleared while they rode under the tarpaulin. The sun was warm on their backs and the country air smelled good.

There were stamping, chomping sounds inside the barn and Tom and Mickey went to investigate. It was dim in the interior, but chinks of light came through the roof and between the loose boards, and at last they made out the shape of a horse standing disconsolately in his stall.

"Hello, there," Mickey said, going up to him. "You look pretty down-in-the-mouth. What's the matter?"

Tom saw the horse's ears flick forward and his head weave from side to side but he couldn't make out a word. "What did he say?" he asked Mickey.

"He said it's a hard life, a hard life," Mickey interpreted. "You're pretty scrawny," he turned to the horse. "Don't you get enough to eat?"

The horse said — according to Mickey — "From *him?* He begrudges every mouthful of hay. He makes me do the work of two horses because he's so stingy."

"Why don't you get out of it once in a while and rest up?" Mickey asked, cocking his head with interest.

The horse said mournfully, "How?"

"Pretend you have a bad limp," Mickey suggested.

"Not a chance," the horse said, with a doleful air. "He'd sell me to the glue factory."

"Oh," said Mickey airily, "as soon as he began talking like *that* you could get over the limp. In the meantime you'd have had a rest."

The horse thought for a moment. "I could try it, I suppose."

"Sure!" Mickey sounded cheerful. "No harm in trying." He leaped up on a stanchion and from there to a rafter. Then he ran crazily along one rafter after another until Tom grew dizzy watching him. "All of 'em rotten," he called down. "It's a wonder the barn holds up! You'd better get out in a hurry," he said to the horse, "if you ever hear anything cracking!"

Tom went and got an apple off the ground. He offered it to the horse; he was sorry for him. The horse looked at him with surprised eyes and then took the apple gingerly from Tom's palm. He chewed it with a wry face. "It's sour," he said gloomily, "and full of worms. But still, it's an apple. I haven't had one in so long I'd forgotten what they taste like."

Mickey slid down the hay pile and then scratched himself. "It prickles," he said. "But it was fun."

They went out into the sunlight, which seemed doubly welcome after the dark old barn. A rooster was crowing in the chicken yard. They went over to look at him. He was a handsome rooster. "At least *he* looks well fed," Tom commented.

Mickey asked the rooster about it. "That man wouldn't give me an extra grain of corn," he said with a toss of his head. "But I'm a good scratcher. I have to be — to take care of all my hens and chickens."

"Are they all yours?" Mickey asked, gazing around at the dozens of brown-feathered chicks busily scratching, too, in the unkempt yard.

"Oh, *he* probably thinks they're his," the rooster

said. "But they are in my care . . . and I do well by them. No better laying hens in the county — so I've heard him say. And knowing him, that's a good deal.

Not that he gives *me* credit, of course." His beady eyes fastened on Tom, then on Mickey. "Where did you come from? Are you going to live here?"

"Gracious, no!" Mickey said violently.

"But then, why did you come?"

"Didn't you ever do anything by mistake?" Mickey asked in turn.

"Oh my, yes," the rooster said. "Many and many a time."

"Well, that's how we got here."

"Then you've come from far away?" the rooster asked.

"It seems like it. . . ."

"You'll be hungry, if you have a long way to go. I will get you something to eat. . . . Betsy!" he called importantly, and a plump brown hen looked up from her scratching.

"Betsy," he said loudly, "go and show these — ah, these friends of mine where two of our best eggs are."

She hesitated a moment. "*He'll* make a frightful to-do about it," she said fearfully.

"Why should he? He doesn't need to know a thing about it. . . . Now hurry, Betsy. The poor things are hungry."

Betsy cast a glance over her shoulder, but the big rooster fixed her with his eye, and she went into the henhouse and led the way to a nest. "Help yourself," she said to Mickey. "But if you ask me, I'd take this one — and this one. . . . They're freshest."

Mickey grabbed them both and put them in the cap. "Did you thank her?" Tom asked.

"Give me time," Mickey said blandly. "You're very beautiful, Betsy," he said then, and Betsy ruffled her feathers and preened before him. "I don't think I ever saw a better-looking hen. And that rooster — I forgot to ask his name — "

"Daniel," said Betsy.

"Daniel. He's really handsome!"

"Yes," said Betsy. "We think so. And so does he, for that matter. He's hard to live with sometimes, he's so *masterful,* always wants his own way. But roosters are like that, and he has his good points. He's bright, too. I don't think *he* will ever catch him!" She sounded very proud and tossed her head, just as Daniel had done, toward the house.

"I'm going to eat my egg right away," Mickey announced. "I'm hungry."

"Oh no, don't!" Tom cried. "We'd better wait."

"If I wait, I'll be still hungrier," said Mickey, and cracked it neatly on the edge of a board. He held it aloft and let the contents dribble into his mouth. Then he smacked his lips. "Umm, delicious!" he said to Betsy.

"Oh, thank you," she cackled happily. "I always do my best."

"I feel better now," Mickey said, as they walked into the barnyard again, and out toward the field. He handed Tom his egg and Tom put it carefully in his pocket where it made quite a bulge. Then Mickey put the cap on again, and as he did so he almost stumbled against a large black and white dog sitting in the sun and scratching himself, first behind his ear, then on his leg, then under his jaw.

"Well, for goodness' sake," Mickey exclaimed, "who are *you?*"

The dog got up but almost immediately sat down again and began biting at himself. "I'm Chump, the watchdog," he announced in a weary, hollow voice.

"Watchdog!" Mickey chortled. "A fine watchdog you are! Why didn't you bark at us?"

"I was busy," Chump said. "And besides, why bother — for *him?*" He cocked his head toward the house. "*I* knew you were here, and *you* knew you were here, and what *he* doesn't know doesn't bother him. So why bark?"

Mickey screwed up his little face in amusement. "That's one way to look at it. But do you know what *I* think?"

"What?"

"I think you don't bark because you're too miserable. What you need is a real going-over; you seem to have a lot of troubles."

Chump said, rolling his mournful eyes upward, "Haven't I! But there's nobody to care but myself."

"Let me help," Mickey offered. "I can't spend very long over it, but every little bit helps." He set down the cap, and leaped onto Chump's back. At once he began searching busily through the dog's hair. "See — here's a flea . . . and here . . . and here. . . . My, my," he shook his head, "it's a wonder you aren't out of your mind!"

He scrabbled up toward Chump's head and worked

there for a while. Chump sat still, a pleased expression coming over his face. Mickey chattered at him, holding up one flea after another. "There! Isn't that better? I could work on you for a week, but with a start like this, maybe you can take over."

Chump got up and stretched himself as Mickey slid quickly to the ground. "I feel like a new dog," he said solemnly. "I wish you could stay on here . . . but I shouldn't wish that on any creature."

Mickey said, "Well, why do *you* stay?"

"I'm too old to start life somewhere else," Chump said. "It might be hard finding enough food."

Mickey flirted his tail with an angry flick. "You *are* a Chump," he said. "Stay here, then. *We* won't, that's sure."

A cow mooed at them from the field and Tom and Mickey wandered over. "Hello, there," Mickey greeted her. "How's the grass?"

The cow stopped chewing and raised her head. "Not too good."

Mickey looked over the wide field. "You have plenty to eat, anyhow."

[50]

"Yes and no," said the cow. "There's not as much grass as there should be, and what there is is full of burdock. Still, my milk's very good. . . . Would you like to try some?"

"Here?" said Mickey in surprise.

"No, no, I never let anyone milk me but the farmer's wife. She's none too gentle, but she's a lot better than *he* is."

Mickey turned to Tom. "Would you like some milk?"

"Yes, I would," Tom said enthusiastically. "I'm thirsty. Where do we get it?"

Mickey asked the cow, and the cow said, "She always puts a big pan of it to cool in the shed next the barn. You'd better hurry — it's almost time for her to take it in. And besides, this is her baking day."

The cow lowered her head and began nosing about in the grass and chewing again.

"Good-by," said Mickey, "and thanks a lot."

"Don't mention it," said the cow. She gave a gusty sigh. "Soon I'll have to stay in that barn again," she said unhappily. "My, how I do hate it."

"Yes," Mickey said, "I can see that. You mean the roof might fall in any minute."

"I never thought about that," the cow said. "I mean that horse. . . . He's so silent. Never a civil word. And when he does talk all he does is complain. It's enough to sour a saint, and I have to stay pleasant on account of my milk."

"We all have our troubles," Mickey said, swinging the cow's tail back and forth.

The cow turned and looked at him. "You?" she said. "You don't have a care in the world."

"I have Dr. Dinkelhofer," Mickey said.

"I don't know him," the cow remarked.

"Then you don't know what trouble is," Mickey told her. "But at that, I'll take him rather than the horse."

Sure enough, on a shelf inside the lean-to was a deep pan full of milk; cream had collected in a thick skin on top, and Tom licked his lips at the prospect of skimming some of it off.

He looked around for something to drink it from. In a corner was an old pot, but it looked rusty. He peered outside. There was a tin cup hanging by a cord from the pump. They could use that.

He went out and got it. Carefully he poured some of the milk into the cup and handed it to Mickey. "You

drink first," he said, feeling very polite. He was *so* thirsty.

Mickey sniffed at it. "Cow's milk! I don't think I like that kind."

"Why," Tom asked in surprise, "what other kind is there?"

"Goat's milk and mare's milk" — Tom made a face — "and monkey's milk, of course. Any of those is better. So you drink this — if you want to."

Tom did want to, very much. He lifted the cup to his lips and a little cool air floated up to him from the milk. But just as he put his mouth to the rim of the cup Mickey cried, "Eeeek!"

"What's the matter?"

"The farmer's wife! She's coming out of the door. And behind her is that man again!"

Chapter Five

THEY DIDN'T STOP RUNNING till the shabby old farmhouse was out of sight and they could feel safe.

Then Tom gave a jaunty whistle and Mickey drew
in a deep breath. "We certainly left *there* in a hurry,
and I'm just as glad of it," he said. "But I'm still
thirsty."

"We'll find a drink." Tom sounded confident.

The day had grown warmer. It was almost too warm to walk. Or maybe that was because they had been running and had had to escape from danger. They were on a country road, and it was pleasant to scuff through the dust and watch it eddy in little swirls about their feet. Tom was enchanted with the tiny footprints Mickey left in the dust. They were neat and delicate and precise, though they zigzagged all over the road as Mickey ran happily from one side to the other. If it weren't for the footprints he would have had a hard time believing that he was really out walking on a country road with a little gray monkey . . . but there he was. And there was Mickey.

Or was he? In that second he had disappeared. "Mickey!" Tom called in a sudden panic. He didn't see him anywhere. "MICKEY! WHERE ARE YOU?"

From the tree almost in front of him came a scratching and hissing and chattering. A plump gray squirrel circled the trunk so fast that all Tom could see was a bit of tail. Behind him came another, larger streak of gray lightning — Mickey. They tore around the trunk in dizzy upward spirals . . . first Tom saw them, then he didn't, then he did. They disappeared among the leaves and the leaves shook and the branches swayed. And after a moment they were both out on a limb, with the squirrel chattering like mad at Mickey and Mickey making faces and chattering back at the squirrel.

The squirrel leaped to the end of a small twig, and it quivered and swayed so violently that Tom was sure it would break off with the squirrel on it. Mickey finally turned his back, swung his tail in an arc, and clambered down the trunk again.

"Silly thing!" Mickey said in disgust. "He acts as if he thought I were a thief!"

"Maybe he was afraid you'd steal some of his nuts — wherever they are," Tom said.

"Pooh!" Mickey mumbled crossly. "He has enough nuts stored in that hole to last for three winters. *He* needn't worry."

Mickey's voice was muffled and indistinct. "*What*

did you say?" Tom demanded. "I can scarcely hear you."

"Well, it's hard to talk with nuts in my cheek."

"Nuts in your cheek! Where did you get them?"

"I picked up a few on my way up — or was it down?" Mickey said. "See?" He opened his mouth and pulled out three nuts, all wet. "Want some?"

"N-no, thank you," Tom said hastily. He thought fast how he could keep from hurting Mickey's feelings. Suddenly his eyes fell on a tree that stood across the road and behind a fence. "Oh, there's a nut tree over there!" he said. "You keep your own and I'll get some of those. They're black walnuts. Best nuts in the world."

Tom went across the road and skinned under the fence. Fortunately there were plenty of nuts lying on the ground, some still green, but some ripe enough to eat. He looked around for two rocks and found them, a flat one to lay the nuts on, a hard round one to smash them with.

"Let's sit down," he suggested, "while I crack the nuts and pick out the meats."

Mickey watched him smashing a nut. It looked easy. "Let me try!"

Tom handed over the rock. Mickey heaved. He heaved again. It took both front paws to lift it and his face puckered with the strain. "Ooof, that's heavy!" he said, breathing hard and letting the rock fall. It slipped off the lower stone and bounced on the end of his tail which was curled around his body.

"Ouch!" Mickey cried loudly and leaped up in the air. He grabbed his tail and looked at it worriedly. His face wore such a comical expression that Tom couldn't help laughing.

"You wouldn't laugh if it were *your* tail!" Mickey chattered at him. "You can smash your own nuts. It's much too hard. And too dangerous."

"I'm sorry I laughed." Tom was contrite. "I know it hurt. . . . Here, taste one of the meats — as soon as I dig it out." He poked industriously with the nail from his pocket, prying out the tiny pieces of nut meat and laying them carefully on a leaf. Mickey picked them up in his fingers and put them tentatively into his mouth.

[59]

He screwed up his eyes and wrinkled his nose. "Ugh!
. . . They make the inside of my mouth draw together!" he cried. "How can you say they're *good?*"
With a vigorous motion he spat them out. "Eat them
yourself. I like the ones the squirrel gathered."

And he cracked them with his strong teeth and ate
them while Tom dug happily in the shells for the hard-
to-get bits that always tasted best.

"It's a good thing I brought this nail with me," he
said with satisfaction. Mickey wanted to know why he
had brought a nail along — it seemed an odd thing to
take to the Zoo. And after all, that's where they had
meant to go; they had never intended to come out into
the country and pry nut meats out of shells.

"Well," said Tom, busily scooping up the bits
that fell onto the ground, "it's for my tree house
really."

"Your tree house?" Mickey echoed. "What's that?
You *have* a house."

"Yes, but that's where I have to live all the time with
my mother and father. The tree house — well, it's in
a tree out in the yard and I can live there by myself

[60]

whenever I want to. I'm building it!" he said proudly. "All by myself, too. It takes time."

"I used to live in the trees," Mickey said slowly, as if he were remembering something from long ago. "All my family did. But not in a house."

Tom looked across at Mickey, his eyes growing wide. "Listen, Mickey, *you* could live in my tree house!" he said excitedly. As he began thinking it out his voice grew louder and his words faster and faster. "You could live there all the time, instead of at Dr. Dinkelhofer's, and you could do just as you please with nobody to watch over you. And I'd live there, too — whenever I could. How about it? Would you like that?"

"Well," said Mickey, "I do like it in trees. I feel at home there." And before Tom could say "Jack Robinson" he had leaped up the trunk of the nut tree and was swinging through the branches with a busy rustling sound. Tom peered upward, trying to see him — he could hear him, but he couldn't locate him. And just then Mickey appeared, halfway to the top, and started out toward the telephone wire.

Tom jumped to his feet, shouting, "Don't, Mickey! Don't!"

Mickey hesitated a moment. "What's the matter? I could travel along fast up here."

"Don't go out on that wire. You'd get burned."

Mickey's incredulous little face peered down at him. "Burned? There isn't any fire."

"But there is — inside. It's electricity. You just take my word for it and don't touch it. Come on down. . . . We'll go on together."

Mickey came slowly down the tree. "*Hmmm,*" he sounded disappointed. "Things are certainly funny. If it has fire in it why don't you see flames? I thought it was a kind of vine that men had."

"It is," Tom said, suddenly. "That's what it is. . . . A kind of vine to carry electricity from one place to another. But it's not for monkeys."

"Why not?" Mickey asked, reasonably enough. "Birds sit on it." And he pointed to a row of small black birds perched like dark clothespins on the wire.

"That's different," Tom said promptly. "But don't ask me why." Come to think of it, why *could* birds sit on a wire sometimes, and not get hurt? He must remember to ask his father about that.

"I'm still hungry," Mickey said suddenly.

"So am I," Tom agreed. He put the nail back in his pocket and picked up a large gnarled stick. It was almost as high as his shoulder, thick and sturdy. "Let's go exploring. We'll pretend we're going through the jungle. You can be the scout and go ahead."

Mickey fell in with the idea in a most satisfactory fashion. He ran forward, peering under his cap right and left, and coming back to report. "Nothing but trees," he said, "and no food anywhere. Fields all dried up. No fruit. Grass shriveled. Lake bed full of dry bones."

Tom pretended to stagger. He mopped his brow and sank down on the ground. "I guess we're done for, pardner," he croaked.

"Don't you believe it!" Mickey chuckled. "Wait till I scout some more." He ran up the nearest tree. "I see a car coming through the jungle."

"A car!" Tom leaped up. "Maybe a Marine in a

jeep! Coming to rescue us! Come down, Mickey, come down. I wouldn't leave the jungle without you!"

Mickey slithered down beside him just as the car drew up. It was a shiny black car, long and low, with a light tan top. A very beautiful lady was driving it.

Chapter Six

Tom DIDN'T EXPECT her to stop, but she did. She leaned out and her hair caught the sunlight. "What a *darling* monkey!" she cried, her eyes dancing. "Is he yours?"

"He's — he's my friend," Tom said.

"Is he a trained monkey? Can he do tricks?"

"Mickey," said Tom proudly, "can do anything."

"Oh, really?" said the lady, her eyes wide. "Do let me see!"

"What does she want to see?" Mickey asked.

"Oh — anything. I told her you could do tricks. Just act like — like a monkey."

Mickey said, "That's easy. It sounds just like Dr. Dinkelhofer. Maybe she's a relative of his. . . . But no, I guess not. She's too pretty. Dr. Dinkelhofer isn't pretty."

He leaped up on Tom's shoulder and made a face at the lady. He tweaked Tom's ear and rumpled his hair. Then, like a gray flash, he scrambled up the tree from which he had first glimpsed the car and crawled out on a limb. Near the end of it he turned a somersault and hung by his tail. The cap fell to the ground beside Tom. Mickey gathered a few maple seed pods and threw them neatly so that they landed on the seat beside the lady. Then he hurried down the trunk, snatched up the cap and, dancing lightly on his tiny feet, he pirouetted around, jumped up on the running board and thrust the cap into her astonished face.

[66]

She clapped her hands. "He's delightful! I think you're the luckiest boy alive. . . . You must be awfully clever to have taught him so many tricks. Here, my dear, this is for you." And she dropped a quarter into the cap.

The car drove off, leaving little spurts of dust. Mickey, squatting in the road, picked the quarter out of the cap and bit it. "It has a funny taste," he told Tom. "You can have it."

"No, it's yours. . . . That's money. It will buy things," Tom told him. "You earned it, so you keep it."

Mickey put the quarter in his cheek and resettled the cap on the back of his neck. "All right. I must say that's an easy way to earn money. Is that how you got yours?"

Tom grinned. "No. Earning money's easy for *you*. I had to do all kinds of things."

"Well, of course, you can't swing by your tail," Mickey said thoughtfully. "My, I've often wondered — what do people *do* without tails? They seem to manage all right, in a way, but it must be an awful nuisance not to have one. I don't know how I'd get along without mine."

Tom considered this. "I suppose tails are all right for monkeys, but not right for people, or they'd have them."

"What did you do to get *your* money?" Mickey came back to the question.

Tom remembered. "Oh, I swept the walks and I gathered some berries this summer, and I cleaned out the cellar, and I walked Mrs. French's dog, and I had a tooth pulled — "

"You got money for having a tooth pulled?" Mickey sounded horrified.

Tom explained. "You see, I didn't want to have it pulled, but it was loose, so Daddy said if I'd let him take it out he'd give me a quarter. So I did. . . . It didn't hurt much."

"I'd rather swing by my tail," Mickey said.

Tom plodded along, putting his stick down solidly at every step. He was beginning to be tired, but he didn't want to say so, because Mickey must be even tireder. Yet the monkey didn't seem to be. He pranced about, cavorted ahead and back again, wound himself around Tom's stick.

"There's a stand down the road," Mickey reported suddenly. "With all kinds of things on it."

"A stand in the *jungle?*" Maybe Mickey was imagining things. Maybe if they had to walk any further without food they'd both have queer notions.

But there it was, just a few steps further on, half hidden by some trees and set back on a grassy bit of lawn littered with dry leaves.

It wasn't a very big stand, but it was piled to overflowing with all kinds of things. A row of huge orange pumpkins stood guard in front, and behind them rose banks of squash and eggplant, baskets of green tomatoes and rosy-cheeked apples, red and green cabbages, stalks of celery, bags of oranges and nuts, jars of honey, and jelly catching the light like rubies.

You could hardly see the proprietor behind his wares. He was a little man, as round as a barrel, with lots of shiny black hair and black, snapping eyes, and big flowing black mustachios. He was sitting with his head resting against the back of the stand and his feet up on the counter.

Mickey leaped onto a mound of oranges and scampered over the boards. When the man saw him his chair crashed forward, his feet came slamming off the counter and he stared, open-mouthed. "How's dis?" he cried in a big hearty voice. "I see t'ings, or is dis a monk'?"

"Of course it's a monkey," Tom said.

"He belongs to you?"

"No," said Tom with reluctance. "I wish he did. We're just friends."

The black-eyed man and the bright-eyed monkey stared at each other; the man scratched his head and Mickey scratched his. The man burst out laughing.

"He look jus' like a monk' my frien' Tony have. Cute like-a dickens. I never see a monk' in country. In city, yes, lots of monks all-a time. W'at you do? You give a show? You make da mon' for your pop?"

"No," Tom said, "we're just out enjoying ourselves. We're hungry, so we thought we'd buy something to eat."

"Sure," said the man, grinning broadly. He winked. "I know. You skip da school wit' your monk'. . . . I no tell! W'at you want — a nice punk'? A big squash? A jar jell'? I got da works!"

Tom took out his money and counted it again. He still had fifty-two cents. He shouldn't spend it all; he ought to have ten cents — or more — in case they could find a bus that would let them on. And something might come up where they'd need money; maybe to telephone or to buy an ice-cream cone.

He cast his eye over the stand. "I'd like two apples, please." They shouldn't cost much. "And — and — let me see. . . . Oh, are those dates over there?"

"Nice fresh dates," the man said. "You want?"

A handful of dates . . . that's what the Arabs ate when they traveled over the desert. They could live a whole day on a few dates. If dates could do that for Arabs, they ought to come in handy on a trip like this. "And a package of dates," he said firmly. "Now, what do you want, Mickey?"

Mickey was scampering over the mound of egg-plants. "I want some bananas," he said.

[71]

"I don't see any," Tom looked around. "Isn't there something else, Mickey?"

"Oh, he has bananas all right," Mickey said. "I smell them."

"Mickey wants some bananas," Tom said. "But I told him there aren't any here. Only he says there are. . . . He's just being funny, I guess." Tom felt that he ought to apologize.

To his surprise the man burst into a roar of laughter. "W'at-a monk'! He sharp like a pin! Sure I got banan'! *He* like a banan', *I* like a banan' — too many people like a banan'. So I hide. I keep under counter, so only I can eat."

"You see?" Mickey said in triumph. He took his quarter out of his cheek. "Here, I'll pay for them myself."

The man's eyes fairly popped. "A monk' wit' a mon'! Now, even in city I never see dis! How you get?"

"Tell him never mind how I got it," Mickey said. "I want some bananas, and this is good money, even if it doesn't taste like it. You said so."

Tom told the man what Mickey had said — but not just the way he had said it. The man chuckled and waggled his mustachios. "A fine monk' he is!" He reached down under the counter and brought up two bananas. "I no sell. No, sir. I give! See, for free!" And he presented them to Mickey with a low bow.

Mickey took them in his hands and stripped off the skins rapidly. He dropped them on the mound of eggplants and Tom snatched them up and looked around for a place to deposit them. "Here," said the man, "I fix." He threw them into an empty basket. Fascinated, then, he watched Mickey eat the bananas. They disappeared like magic.

"Ummm," said Mickey, wiping his mouth, "I haven't tasted anything so good in days!" And he jumped across to the man's shoulder and put his arms around his neck.

Tom paid for his purchases. They came to twenty-nine cents, and he was counting his change when Mickey shrieked, "There! See it? There's a coconut!"

"How much is it?" Tom asked.

"Oh," said the man, still beaming from the monkey's hug, "how I know? Is last one left. Five cent — ten cent — what you like."

Mickey was clutching the coconut to him like a long-lost friend. Five cents or ten cents — how did you settle a problem like that? Maybe sort of halfway between would be right. Carefully Tom counted out eight cents. The man didn't even seem to notice.

"How I wish I had a monk' like him!" the man

sighed, rolling his eyes fondly at Mickey. "His little paw, his soft fur, his funny face. You sell him?" he asked hopefully.

"No, no!" Tom said hurriedly. "He doesn't belong to me. He's just a friend. . . . We have to be going now."

"He is quick like a flash. I get lonely here; is not'ing to do. I like a monk' to keep me company. He is good company, no?"

"He's lots of fun," Tom said with warmth. "He can do all kinds of things. And he talks, too."

The minute he had said it he knew he should not have said it.

"Ha-ha, ha-ha, ha-ha!" the man laughed. He opened his mouth wide, showing all his teeth. He rocked his head. He held his sides. "Sure, sure! I talk Italiano. What he talk — Americano, Chinese, French? I bet we onderstan' each other!"

Tom said quickly, "Come along, Mickey. . . . We still have a long way to go."

Mickey hopped off the orange crate and put the coconut in his cap. "What are we waiting for?"

"Good-by," Tom said politely to the man, who was still laughing. "And thank you very much."

The man waved to them. "Good-by — you come back. I give him all the free banan' he want. A monk' who talk!" He yelled after them, "You want to sell him one day, you tell me — I buy him quick like dat!"

Chapter Seven

Tom could hardly wait to get away from the place. The man was nice enough, but he had been so taken with Mickey that if they had stayed around there was no telling what he might do. He half ran down the road, with Mickey staggering along beside him.

"Hey, wait a minute," Mickey panted. "I can't —

keep up — with you. This coconut weighs — almost as much — as I do."

Tom felt contrite. "It's only till we get out of sight," he told Mickey. "Then we can sit down and rest, and work on the coconut. That was a bright idea of yours, to get a coconut. I never would have thought of it."

"That's because you aren't a monkey," Mickey said with a sort of smug air.

"It's going to take a lot of working on," Tom said thoughtfully. "It's awfully hard to get a coconut open. . . . I know, because I've watched Mother. Sometimes she puts it in the oven to crack it, but of course we have no oven here."

"Pooh," said Mickey. "We don't need one. It'll open as easy as pie."

"I'd carry it for you," Tom offered, "but I have all this other stuff. I'll tell you what! You carry the apples and the dates and I'll take your cap and the coconut."

"No, you won't," Mickey said. "You've been trying to get that cap all along. Besides, it makes a very good thing to carry the coconut in. Only," he sighed, "it seems to be getting heavier and heavier."

"Here," said Tom, "we can sit down now." They had passed a bend in the road and he felt it was safe. There was a spreading tree and a patch of shade beneath it. "Now you wait till I get out my knife and I'll see if I can pry it open."

Mickey said scornfully, "People always want to do things the hard way."

"But you have to," Tom said, "on a coconut."

"No such thing," said Mickey. He put the cap on the ground, grabbed the coconut in the crook of one arm, and clambered up the tree trunk. He was a little slow this time because of the weight in his arm, but even so he disappeared while Tom was blinking at him. "You go up to a nice high branch," he called back, "and you crawl out as far as you can, so you're clear, and then you drop it — WHAM — like this."

The coconut fell with a SPLAT almost at Tom's feet — and in the twinkling of an eye Mickey was down again. "And there it is, cracked as neatly as you please. A good job if I do say so myself."

Tom started to pick it up. "Watch out, watch out!" Mickey chattered. "Don't spill the milk in it!"

But it was too late. Tom had already lifted it, and the coconut fell apart in five pieces. The delicious fluid drained away on the road, spreading into the dust.

"Now see what you've done!" Mickey scolded.

"And it would have tasted so good!" Tom mourned.

"Oh well, we can eat the coconut anyhow," Mickey said with a cheerful air. He took up one of the smaller pieces and began chewing on it busily. "I picked a good one," he commented.

Tom thought they might as well make the best of a bad thing and sat down under the tree and fished in his pocket for his knife. He was glad he had brought it with him, even if the blade was rather dull and not much good. He wedged it between the milk-white meat and the brown hairy shell and finally worked a small piece loose.

"Gnaw it, gnaw it!" Mickey said with impatience, glancing over at him with his little bright eyes. "What do you have teeth for?"

"To chew with," Tom answered, grinning.

"Well, that's not all they're for," Mickey told him. "People clutter themselves up with a lot of things they don't need. You don't have to use a knife — see, just gnaw it out like this!" And he held a piece of coconut shell up to his face, bit into it, and a piece of white meat came away neatly. "I'll have this all eaten before you've got yourself one little bite."

They sat companionably side by side, chewing on the sweet coconut meat. "The more you chew, the better it tastes," Tom commented.

Mickey's eyes snapped. "And the more you eat, the better you feel."

Tom laughed, for he saw that all of Mickey's share of the coconut was gone. "I know what you mean! Here, have some dates."

After they had done away with the dates, Tom brought out the apples. He bit into his. It was a very good apple, tart and juicy.

Mickey tasted a piece. "I don't care much for apples." He tossed his under a bush.

"Don't you *like* it?" Tom asked, unbelieving.

[81]

"Bananas are better. . . . Why don't you eat your egg?"

Tom got it out and looked at it. He was surprised that it didn't have a crack. It must have a good hard shell.

"I'd have to cook it first," he said. "You know — fry it on the sidewalk, only it isn't hot enough to do that and there aren't any sidewalks out here, or boil it in water, only we haven't any water."

"Not to mention a fire," said Mickey. "Eat it raw."

Tom shook his head. Just thinking about it made him feel queasy, and he wished he hadn't mentioned water. "I — I think I'll just take it home to Mother. As a sort of present."

He thought that it might be a very wise idea to take a present to his mother. He had been gone a long time, and she didn't know where he was. As a matter of fact, he didn't, either, but he was sure he would get home eventually.

Just the same, it might help matters to take his mother a gift when he explained what had happened

on this amazing day. Would she like an egg? He hoped
so. She would certainly have plenty of uses for it. He
had never brought her an egg as a present before, but
this was different. This was a very special egg — from
Betsy and Daniel.

After a while they felt rested. Tom stowed his stuff
and they started out again. His pockets bulged alarm-
ingly, for he had decided to keep the biggest piece of
coconut shell — they might have a use for it — and
anyhow, what were pockets for?

The road stretched ahead as far as they could see.
"Are we still in the jungle?" Mickey asked.

"No," said Tom, brightening, as he saw a picture in
his mind's eye. This was an adventure. "We're in the
desert now. The sun's beating down on us and we're
looking for water. We've been marching for days and
days and days. If we could just find water, we'd be all
right. Do you see any, Mickey?"

Why hadn't he thought to ask the lady for a ride?
She had had a whole empty seat; she could have taken
them back to town, or wherever she was going. Of

course, he wasn't supposed to hitch rides, ever. But he could at least have asked her if they were on the right road to town, and how far it was. And why hadn't he asked the Italian for a drink? He *was* thirsty.

Mickey was running ahead, his hand to the visor of the cap, peering diligently right and left. Then he came racing back.

"No water," he said. "It just looked like it in the road."

"A mirage," Tom said importantly. He had read about mirages. You thought you saw a shining pool of lovely cool water, but when you got up to it, it was just sand again . . . and further on, you thought you saw another pool.

All at once Tom thought of his roll of peppermints. He had forgotten about them. He pulled them out and undid the paper and foil wrappings. "Here," he said, "maybe one of these will help."

Mickey took one of the smooth white candy circles with the hole in it and examined it carefully. He turned it about and put it up to his eye, and tossed it from one hand to the other and smelled it. "I don't see how this can help." He looked up at Tom, puzzled. "It's not a drink."

"Pop it in your mouth — like this — you'll see," Tom showed him.

Mickey, still looking unbelieving, popped it into his mouth. He sucked at it, as Tom was doing, and cocked his head. The taste seemed to please him and he drew in his breath. The expression that came over his face then was so funny that Tom laughed aloud. He knew what had happened. The air on the peppermint had made a coldness in Mickey's mouth, but it was such a strange, new feeling that Mickey was entranced.

He opened his mouth and took the peppermint out again in his fingers, turning it about and staring at it.

"Where does the cold come from?" he asked.

"It's the air," Tom said grandly, but he wasn't quite sure.

"The air isn't cold — outside," Mickey protested. "But when it gets in my mouth, it is." He twisted the peppermint about again — and dropped it in the road.

"Have another one," Tom said.

But quick as a wink Mickey had stooped and picked

it up. He wiped it off in a careless fashion and put it into his mouth again. "Pooh," he said, "what's a little dust?" He sucked in his breath with a long Oo-oo-oo. The wonderful sensation was still there. His eyes crinkled and he grinned.

"What did you call these?" he asked. Tom told him.

"Pep-per-mints," Mickey said slowly. "Pep-per-mints. I must remember that. I wonder if Dr. Dinkel-hofer has any around the house?"

Chapter Eight

I'VE WORN the soles off my feet," Mickey remarked.

"Do they hurt? Do you want to ride on my shoulder?" Tom asked with concern. His own feet hurt, but *he* had shoes on, and he was so much bigger and stronger.

[87]

Just then Tom thought he saw the roof of a farmhouse rising above the trees. "When we get there I'll ask for a drink," he said to himself. He didn't say it out loud, because he didn't know what they would find and he didn't want Mickey to feel badly.

The farmhouse came nearer and nearer, and Tom was glad because his throat was parched and his tongue felt as if it were made of fur.

But when they came close, he saw that it had a deserted look. Not as if the people were gone for the day, but as if no one at all lived there. There was a sort of *still* air about the place, and the doors and windows were all closed and the blinds were drawn halfway at all the windows. His heart sank but he went up to the front door and knocked anyway.

There was no answer. Not even a dog barked. He waited awhile and then went around to the back. It was quiet and closed up there, too. Just as he was about to turn away he noticed that there was a well in the yard.

A well! That meant water! But there was no bucket standing by, nor a dipper, nor anything they could use to draw up the water.

He licked his dry lips. Here was water . . . and nothing to get it with.

But wait! The piece of coconut shell! He *knew* he had brought it with a reason. It was almost like a shallow bowl. It would make a wonderful dipper.

He got out his nail, with a triumphant glance at Mickey, and hammered a small hole in each side of the shell with a flat rock. Then he fished around in his pocket for the piece of string, knotted it carefully on either side of the shell, cut it off with his knife, and attached the rest of the string by a knot to the middle of the crosspiece. He hoped it would be long enough to let down into the water.

Tom shoved the wooden cover aside and peered over the edge. Mickey jumped up on the coping and peered in, too. They could see the water not too far below and their own dark reflections in it. Mickey made faces at himself and pranced about on the coping, watching his reflection do the same.

[89]

"Don't fall in," Tom cautioned, carefully paying out the string.

"Don't fall in yourself," Mickey retorted. "Will it reach?"

Anxiously Tom let out a foot more and a foot more, keeping a worried eye on the string still in his hand. It went almost to the last inch . . . and then the coconut shell rested on the water. Tom leaned over and let out the last bit of string. But the shell did not sink beneath the water. It stayed there on top, dry and empty.

He felt so disappointed that he wanted to stamp his foot. There was the water, and there was the shell to drink out of, but the shell wouldn't go beneath the water. And why not? Suddenly he gave such a whoop that Mickey tumbled backwards. "It's too light!" Tom shouted. "That's why. It's too light!"

Mickey righted himself and said crossly, "It's always light in the daytime. What's the matter with you?"

"I'm a dumb bunny, that's what I am," Tom said, hardly hearing Mickey.

"Well, you said it, I didn't."

"We have to weight it," Tom said, thinking out loud. "So it'll sink. There ought to be plenty of stones around. . . . Mickey, go get me some stones, heavy, but not too big. And clean."

Mickey leaped off the coping. "Why clean ones?"

"Because they're going in the water."

"Then they'll *get* clean," Mickey observed. But he began searching over the ground and the driveway for stones, and soon was back with one in each hand. "Like this?"

"Fine," said Tom, pulling up the shell again. "Maybe three or four more like it will do the trick."

He wiped them off on his trousers and laid them in the shell. Mickey scurried about, muttering to himself. "Seems to me I've walked on all the stones in the world today," he said, "and now I can't find any." Still, he did manage to bring back two more that were not too big, and Tom arranged them close together in the bottom of the shell.

"Now we'll try again," he said hopefully, and payed out the string once more.

[91]

They leaned over the coping, watching, and when the shell came to the water and sank beneath it, Tom let out another shout. Mickey screwed up his face. "I hope you get over this yelling pretty soon," he grumbled. "You hurt my ears."

"But it's water — now we'll have water!" Tom said excitedly.

"It'll still be water if you're still," Mickey said. "What you would do in a jungle I hate to think. You'd make so much racket all the creatures in the place would come running and get the water instead of you."

"But we're not in the jungle," Tom said reasonably.

"That's right — it's the desert. . . . Aren't you going to drink it?" Mickey asked then. His tone was eager. He never stayed cross very long.

"You first," Tom said. It cost him a real effort. He was so thirsty that he would have liked to put his whole face in the shell and gulp down the water to the last drop. He held out the coconut half to Mickey. "Here," he said, squeezing his eyelids shut, "drink all you want."

Mickey held the shell daintily between his front paws and sipped the water in little sips. Tom could hear him. "Don't drink too much," he cautioned.

"How much is too much?" Mickey asked, going right on. "I always drink till I'm not thirsty."

"If you haven't had water for a long time it makes you sick if you take too much at first." Tom thought he had read that somewhere, but he wasn't sure where.

"It only *seems* like a long time," Mickey said. "Now it's your turn."

The shell was quite empty and Tom let it down into the water again, while Mickey wiped his mouth with his hand and looked very pleased.

It tasted even better to Tom than he had imagined it would. It was wonderful . . . no taste at all, really, yet the best in the world. Cool and delicious, moistening his dry lips and his dry mouth and trickling down his dry throat in a lovely cold stream that sent little shivers of pleasure down his back.

He drank three shells full. "I thought you said — " Mickey began, and Tom said guiltily:

"I know. . . . But it's so good. I don't think anything that tastes that good can do any harm, do you?"

Mickey chuckled. "You'll get around to my way of thinking, after all."

"Just the same," Tom said, "it's a lucky thing I had my knife and the string and the nail. We wouldn't have had any water if I hadn't had my knife and the string and the nail."

"We wouldn't have had any of it without the coconut, either," Mickey retorted. "And that was *my* idea."

Chapter Nine

Toм suddenly lifted his head and stood listening. "What's that?"

There was the sound of bells — not musical bells, but all jumbled together in a harsh, familiar way. A wagon loomed into view. The bony horse plodded with slow steps down the dusty road, the driver sat slumped forward with the reins slack in his hands.

Across the middle of the wagon was suspended a row of cowbells and they jangled loudly to the slow movement of the cart.

"A junk wagon!" Tom cried, his eyes alight. "Come on, Mickey, maybe we can hitch a ride!"

They raced forward without a backward glance at the deserted farmhouse, and Mickey, with a light bound, was sitting on top of the junk pile before Tom had managed to hoist himself up. It was higher than he had thought and he landed asprawl in a nest of cans and bottles. Something rolled out of his pocket as he leaped, and fell with a cracking sound on the road. He looked back from his perch. It was the egg! The egg that was to have been a present to his mother.

"You see?" Mickey grinned at him. "You should always eat things like that right away."

Tom was all ready to explain to the driver why they were hitching a ride, but the driver did not even turn, and it dawned on Tom that he must be asleep.

Tom was supposed never, *never* to hitch a ride on a

moving truck or car. He had promised his parents that. But this wasn't a truck or a car. It was a wagon . . . and hardly a *moving* wagon at that.

It was interesting on top of the wagon, once he had had a chance to catch his breath and look around. A fine collection of junk. A wonderful collection of junk! It would be fun to be a junkman's son and have the pick of all the treasures he brought home every day! *His* father was only an engineer.

Mickey was busily rummaging among the odds and ends. "What does he do with all this stuff?" he asked Tom.

"He buys it from people," Tom answered.

"What for?"

"Because they don't want it any more."

"But what does *he* want with it then?"

"He sells it."

Mickey shook his head. "It sounds crazy. If people don't want it, how can he sell it?"

"Well, you see," Tom said slowly, thinking it out, "he buys it from people who don't want it, so he can sell it to people who do."

Mickey was hardly listening. "Eeek! Look what I've found!" he chattered. He was holding out a piece of cracked mirror, turning and twisting it in the light, and blinking at himself in a fascinated sort of way.

"That's a little pocket mirror," Tom told him. "Now if you only had a pocket — "

[98]

"It would fall out and get broken, like your egg," Mickey said. "I'll carry it in my cap . . . after I get done looking in it. Want to see yourself?"

"No," said Tom. "I have to stare in a mirror every day to see if my hair's combed right and my face is washed and all that. . . . Oh look, Mickey, here's something really good! A hinge! Two hinges!"

Mickey wasn't very interested. "What are hinges?"

Tom explained. "I could use these on my tree house. On *our* tree house," he corrected. "You're going to live in it, too. In fact, it will really be *your* house when I finish it, because I won't be able to be there all the time, but you will." He put the hinges in his pocket. Maybe it was just as well that he had lost the egg, for now he had room for the hinges.

He scrabbled happily through the pile. There were all kinds of things he didn't want — parts of an old stove, and a piece of rusty radiator, and broken bottles and bundles of rags and newspapers. But there *were* odd nails and a brown crock and a little chair he could polish or paint. Of course they would be hard to carry.

And he also had to think of his money. He didn't know how much these treasures would cost and he had only twenty-three cents left.

Mickey was playing with his mirror; there was nothing else that interested him so much.

The horse stopped suddenly and Tom, startled, looked up. They had turned off the dusty road onto a paved street with houses and shops and trees. Now that there was no jangle of bells, the driver woke up with a jerk and looked around. His mouth fell open when he saw them.

"Where in tarnation did you come from?" he demanded. But he didn't sound angry. Just puzzled. Perhaps he thought he was still dreaming.

Tom hastened to explain. "We would have asked you for a ride, but you were asleep, I guess. Anyhow, we're getting off here. It was awfully nice of you to let us ride on your wagon this far."

"Haw!" said the junkman. "No 'let' about it. You just rode."

"You don't mind, do you?" Tom asked anxiously. "We were pretty tired. And it was a very nice ride.

We didn't take anything. That is, we found a couple of things we'd like to buy, if I can afford them. These — hinges," he pulled them out with difficulty from his pocket where they were caught, "and this pocket mirror that Mickey wants. How much would they be?"

"Mickey?" the junk dealer repeated. "Who's that?"

"He's my friend," Tom said, and gestured toward Mickey. The man wheeled around in the other direction, and saw Mickey for the first time. "Well, I'll be blowed! Was he here all the time, too?"

"Yes."

The man rubbed his chin on which a stubble of whiskers grew. "Well, I'll be blowed!" he said again. "You two run away from a circus or something?"

"No," said Tom, "we're just out for the day."

"I'll bet you are!" The man burst into a surprising laugh. Mickey jumped, and the horse flicked his ears. "So you caught me napping, heh? For that you can have the stuff for twenty cents. Okay?"

Twenty cents. It seemed like a lot. That would leave him only three cents. Then he couldn't get anything else, but maybe it was just as well. And they *were* good hinges and Mickey was entranced with his mirror. Besides, they had had the ride on the junk wagon.

"Okay," he said, and fished out two dimes. The man bit them. "So long," he said. "I got business here. You sure you didn't take anything else?"

At sight of Tom's face he added hastily, "Forget it. I guess the twenty cents would cover it, anyhow."

Tom and Mickey scrambled off the wagon, and the man got down stiffly, too, and disappeared toward the back of a house. Tom ran to the corner and looked at the sign. Field Avenue, it said. Oh, then he knew where he was. On the edge of town, and about a mile from his home. With a little luck they'd get there pretty soon, if their feet held out. It was a good thing they had had this rest; that was a help.

He began thinking of what he'd do when he got home. There would be a lot of work to be done on the tree house if he and Mickey were to live there. But now that he had these hinges . . . He would make a door, and they'd have a little porch. Mickey could sleep inside at night and in the daytime they'd play together and go adventuring and cook their meals. . . .

"I could forage for our food," Tom said, thinking out loud. "When you live in our tree house, Mickey, you won't have to go hungry. I'll see that you have plenty to eat. Besides bringing you stuff from the house, I could get things with my slingshot."

"What's a slingshot?" Mickey asked.

"Don't you know what a slingshot is?" He extracted it from his bulging pocket and showed it to Mickey.

"I don't get it," Mickey said, scratching his head. "What do you do with it? How does it work?"

"Well, you see," Tom said importantly, "you have to have something to put in it. *This* is the sling part. . . . You have to have the shot part, too. You use stones. Or marbles. That's why I always carry marbles along — besides for play, of course." With some trouble he brought out a marble and, with Mickey's bright eyes watching him, he inserted it in the sling. "Then you aim, see — like this — and pull back — "

With the words there was a loud CRASH, tinkle, tinkle, tinkle, and Tom jumped. Mickey fled in fright.

"Mickey!" Tom shouted, feeling frightened himself. At that moment a heavy hand fell on his shoulder, and a policeman, large and beefy and very red in the face, loomed beside him.

"So *you're* the wan!" he bellowed. "Caught you this time! With the weapon and all and all, right in your wicked hand!"

Chapter Ten

Tom looked down. The slingshot *was* in his hand.
"Wh-what happened?"

" 'What happened?' he says," the policeman mim-
icked. " 'What happened?' he wants to know, like
the innocent lamb he is not. A store window's broke

in a dozen pieces, that's what, my fine lad, and you'll go marching off with me to the jail, that's what, and I'll be taking your weapon from you *if* you please, that's what."

"But I didn't!" Tom found his voice, and it was surprisingly loud. He stared where the policeman pointed and there was a broken plate glass window. "I didn't break it — why, look, the marble's still in my sling!"

"And a lot that means to me! What's to prevent you havin' pulled a fast one before I came up?"

"But I tell you — " Tom protested angrily. And just then there was another CRASH, tinkle, tinkle, tinkle, tinkle . . . and Tom's eyes, darting to the store window, saw that it was broken still further. It was broken into fifty pieces now.

"Now, who did *that*?" the policeman cried. His face was purple. He looked about to burst. But he knew it couldn't have been Tom who had done it. He still had him by the collar, the slingshot was still in full view, unused. With a snort of rage, he released Tom and dashed back toward the store.

[106]

Tom ran. He ran as he never had run before, down the street, around the corner. Mickey appeared at his side as if by magic. He didn't have time to ask where he had been. He was just glad he was safe.

"Wow!" Tom gasped. "Who *do* you suppose broke that window?"

"I don't know who did it the first time, but I did it the second time," Mickey said modestly.

Tom stopped short. "*You* did?"

"Sure. After all, it couldn't hurt it by then, it was all broken anyhow, and I thought if I could keep the policeman from nabbing you — I just shied a stone at it, and I've got a pretty good pitch, if I do say so myself!"

Tom squeezed Mickey's little hand. "You're a grand friend," he said warmly. He was more relieved than he'd like anybody to know. That had been a pretty bad moment back there, with the slingshot in his hand, and the policeman grabbing his shoulder, and the crash of falling glass . . .

It would be exciting to think about tomorrow, perhaps, and to talk about. But right now he wished his heart would quiet down a little.

Mickey limped along beside him. "My feet hurt," he said in an apologetic voice. "I'm not used to walking. It's really a lot easier to swing along in the trees, but you can see that things aren't arranged here for a monkey."

"You get along all right," Tom said with admiration. "I'm sorry about your feet, though. We'll be home soon. . . . I know where we are now." He'd be glad to get home himself.

They walked along like the good companions they were, Tom swinging Mickey's arm, and Mickey chattering beside him. The sun had sunk behind the hills and the air was gray and hazy with leaf smoke and there was a little chill in it. It wasn't cold . . . just the kind of coolness that made you think of a fire and a nice hot dinner and a soft chair and lamps lighted. They were coming nearer and nearer, and he hastened his steps a little.

"Not much further, Mickey," he kept encouraging him. His own feet hurt, and in spite of all he'd eaten he was terribly hungry.

The houses were all familiar now. This was within his own neighborhood; a block or so and they'd be home.

There was the roar of a big motor behind them and a cloud of gasoline fumes. A bus slid to a stop beside them, and Tom saw that it was the one they had tried to board that morning.

[109]

The driver had recognized them. "So!" he yelled. "Here you are! Where's my cap, you rapscallion, you? Where's my cap?" He started down the steps toward them.

Mickey whipped it off his head, and there was the sound of glass breaking at their feet. With an expert toss, Mickey threw the cap at the driver and it landed rakishly over one of his ears.

Somehow that seemed to make the bus driver angrier than if he hadn't got it back at all, and Tom and Mickey put on one last burst of speed. They zipped around the corner, and down half a block, and through Tom's garden gate.

The bus hadn't followed them. The driver was nowhere to be seen. Everything was quiet. There were lights in the living room and the smell of coffee and apple pie floated out to them as they scurried around the house and fell in a heap at the foot of the tree where Tom was building his tree house.

For a little while they just sprawled there, getting back their breath and being glad they had escaped.

"My mirror!" Mickey broke the silence. He sounded mournful. "My mirror fell out and broke. I liked that mirror."

"Never mind, I'll get you another. Mother has lots of them. Or I'll buy you one. A better one."

"Well," said Mickey, "that's nice. I'd like to have something to show for the day. It was quite a day, wasn't it?"

Tom said with great satisfaction, "Quite a day. We'll

have a lot more, Mickey. When you live in the tree
house — "

"By the way," Mickey interrupted, "where *is* this
tree house I'm to live in?"

Tom pointed. "Up there. See it?"

Mickey squinted through the branches. "I see a
couple of boards — "

"That's the floor," Tom said proudly. "It's as far as I've got. But you can sleep on that tonight, and I'll work on it every chance I have and build it good and strong for you, like I said, with a door and windows and a porch and everything. There'll even be steps going up!"

"I don't need steps," Mickey said. His voice sounded little and rather forlorn. "But — if you don't mind, I think I'll go back to Dr. Dinkelhofer's tonight."

Tom cried out in disappointment, "Oh, Mickey!"

"Well," said Mickey, "he'll wonder where I am, and anyhow, it's chilly out here. I'm used to a heated room, you see, and a nice soft bed."

Tom thought about it. He liked a heated room, too, on a cold night, and a nice soft bed. "But you'll come back, Mickey? You'll surely come back so we can play together in the tree house?"

"Oh, I'll come back!" Mickey said quickly and reassuringly. "I'll be seeing you again. Now that I know how easy it is to get out, I'll keep in practice."

He leaped to Tom's shoulder, ran a tiny, delicate

finger along his eyebrows so that it tickled, and blew in his ear.

"Besides, I like you," he said softly.

And then he was gone.

Tom went slowly into the house. The lights made

him blink a little. His mother was opening the oven door to peer at her pie. "Why, Thomas Ashby Evans!" she cried when she saw him. "Where in the *world* have you been?"

Tom knew that his shoes were dusty and his shirt was dirty and there were bits of straw and leaves on his trousers and his hair was mussed. But he knew that his mother was glad to see him, in spite of her voice, just as he was glad to be home.

"I've been to the Zoo," he said.

"To the Zoo!" she echoed. "But you didn't go with your class. Do you mean to say you went alone?"

"No," he said, "I went with Mickey."

"And who is Mickey?"

"He's my friend."

"I don't remember hearing of a Mickey."

"He's a monkey," Tom said. "He's the best friend I ever had."

His mother shot him an amused glance and set the pie on the table. It was brown and crusty and smelled of cinnamon and sugar. "I suppose," she said, "that next you'll be telling me you spent the day with a monkey and had a lot of adventures!"

"Yes," said Tom, "that's just what we did."

"What an imagination!" his mother laughed. "Now run and wash up, dear. Supper's almost ready."

But he *hadn't* imagined it. It had been as real as real. He thought of all the things they had done together and the adventures they had had. But how could he prove it to his mother? The bus driver's cap was given back; and the egg he was going to bring as a present had spilled in the road; and the food they had bought was all eaten; and the coconut shell had been left at the deserted farm. How could he ever prove to his mother that they had done all the things that he would tell her about?

"Mother," he said suddenly, "where does Dr. Dinkelhofer live?"

"What a queer name, dear! I never heard of a Dr. Dinkelhofer."

But there *must* be one! Mickey had said so. Mickey lived there. And Mickey had said that as soon as he could get out he would come again. Tom remembered the feeling of the soft little finger across his eyebrow and the soft little whisper in his ear. Even if his mother thought it was all his imagination, *he* know that Mickey was real, and if Mickey said he would come again, he would.

He whistled happily as he went upstairs to wash his face and get ready for supper.

THE END